The tales of Marty mouse

Contents:-

The tales of Marty mouse.

The
Field of Gold

Marty surveyed the valley in front of him. In the distance he could see a golden glow in the sky, the glow was coming from the field of gold.

'Right, today's the day,' Marty told himself and he ran off to find his best friend Sheldone snail.

Arriving at Sheldone's house, Marty knocks loudly on the door 'Knock, knock'.
'Are you there Sheldone?' he shouts.

The front door opens slowly and standing there in a pair of red and blue pyjamas is a sleepy-looking Sheldone.

'Oh, It's you Marty' he says yawning 'What are you doing here?'

''I'm going on an adventure and I wondered if you wanted to come with me? said Marty excitedly.

'An adventure to where?' asks Sheldone yawning.

'I'm going to the field of gold' Marty said confidently.
'The field of gold, you're really going to the field of gold?' asked Sheldone trying to contain his excitement.

Since they were little they had been told the stories of the infamous field of gold and how nobody had been brave enough to go there.

'Are we really going to the field of gold?' asked Sheldone.

'Yep' replied Marty.

'Can Wallace come with us?' asks Sheldone.

'As soon as you're ready, we'll go and see him' said Marty reminding Sheldone he is still wearing his pyjamas.

Sheldone goes inside to change. Moments later he reappears and they head off towards the home of Wallace worm.

Arriving at Wallace's front door Marty knocks loudly 'Knock, knock'.

An upstairs window opens.

'Who's that banging on my door?' shouts a grumpy Wallace.

'It's us' they reply.

'Do you want to come on an adventure with us?' asks Marty.

'What sort of adventure?' enquires Wallace.

Sheldone interrupts, 'We're going to the field of gold'.

The mention of the field of gold brings a smile to Wallace's face.

'The field of gold! You bet, you can count me in' he said.

'Great' replied Marty, 'Meet us down by the river in an hour' he added.

'And bring some lunch with you' adds Sheldone.
An hour later they meet on the river bank.

Marty orders Sheldone and Wallace to go and find the biggest leaf they can.

'What's the leaf for?' asks Wallace.

'It's going to carry us across the river' replied Marty, 'So make sure it big enough and strong enough to carry all of us'.

Sheldone and Wallace disappear into the woods. Marty searches for twigs they can use as oars.

After a few minutes Sheldone and Wallace return dragging a very large leaf from a near by oak tree.

'Will this do?' they ask.

'Let's find out' said Marty dragging the leaf into the water.

'Hooray' shouts Wallace, 'It floats'.

Gingerly they climb into the makeshift boat.

'It's a bit wobbly' says Sheldone, struggling to keep his balance.

'Hold on tight' yells Marty.

The makeshift boat rocks from side to side.

'We're not going to make it' shouts a worried Wallace.

'We'll make it' says Marty reassuringly. They battle the strong wind and finally reach the other side.

'Phew, that was scary' says Sheldone stepping out of the boat.

Exhausted they decide to rest and eat their lunch.

Marty tucks into a big double layered cheese sandwich, which he has cut into triangles.

Sheldone has made a large lettuce roll.

Whilst Wallace tucks into a very messy mud sandwich.

Stomachs full, they decide to take a short nap.

Once refreshed they begin their long trek towards the farmer's field.

They climb the muddy bank, fight their way through the tall grass and make their way across the open woodland.

It's then that Marty stops in his tracks.

'There it is' he yells pointing skywards,

'There's the gold'.

Sheldone and Wallace strain their necks as they look skywards.

Wallace gulps.

'That's extremely high' he says.

Sheldone steps forward flexing his muscles. 'Leave this to me' he said, 'I'll give the stem a good shaking'.

He steps forward and shakes the stem with all his strength, but nothing happens.

'Let me have a go' says Wallace.

He also gives the stem a good shake and again nothing happens.

'We'll never get that down' he said.

'Oh, yes we will' says Marty, 'I'll climb it' he said.

So he steps forward and grabs hold of the stem and In no time at all he has made it to the top.

'I can see it' he shouts.

He leans across and with one hand he tries to grab hold of the gold.

'Can you reach it?' asks Sheldone.

Marty tries again. This time he uses both hands. The piece of gold comes free. He then realises that he has let go of the stem, both he and the gold come crashing to the ground.

His concerned friends come to his aid.

'Are you OK?' they ask.

Marty is sat shaking his head, 'I think so' he said.

Wallace points to the piece of gold lying next to him on the ground.

'Yippee' he shouts, 'We've done it, we've got the gold'.

They begin celebrating.

'I can't wait to tell everyone' says Wallace.

'We'd better head home now' said Sheldone.

They gather their treasure and head back to the boat and make their way back across the river.

On reaching the other side Marty jumps out of the boat with the gold.

'Come on you two' he shouts over his shoulder as he runs towards home.

Sheldone and Wallace follow.

Out of breath they enter through the front door.

'Mum, Dad, look what we've got?' he announces putting the gold on the kitchen table.

His parents notice the piece of corn.

'It's gold' says Wallace.

'I'm sorry to tell you that it's not gold, it's corn' said Marty's dad.

'Not gold?' says Marty puzzled, 'But everyone told us that the farmer's field was full of gold'.

'The field is full of corn' explains his Mum, 'To us animals that is as precious as gold, without the corn we would starve'.

She can see the disappointment on their faces.

'Tell you what, why don't I bake you a crusty corn pie for you?'

'Oh, yes please' they reply licking their lips.

Twenty minutes later there is a
steaming hot pie on the kitchen table.

'What a way to end a great adventure'
says Sheldone.

Up, up
and away.

Today is the day the valley holds it's annual kite competition and while most of the valley's residents are still tucked up in their nice cosy beds, Marty is already downstairs working on his design.

Dabbing paint here and there he adds the finishing touches to his kite. Placing it on the kitchen table he stands back and admires his work.

'It's going to take a very special kite to beat this one' he thought to himself.

He looks out of the window to check the weather. It's sunny with a slight breeze. Perfect he thought.

The breeze carries the delicious aroma of freshly baked cakes. Hattie Hedgehog is also up early, she is making corn cakes and berry tarts for the competition. Marty can't resist investigating.

Peeping through her kitchen window, Marty can see a table full of small cupcakes but sat proudly on the sideboard is a large corn and berry cake.

This is the prize for today's winner.

'Wow' says Marty licking his lips, 'I hope I win today'.

He leaves Hattie to her baking and decides to go and check on his competition for this special prize. Three others also want to win the prize.

First he arrives at Sheldone's house, he knocks on the door.

'Are you there, Sheldone?' he asks.

'Yes' came the reply 'But you can't come in as I'm still working on my design'.

'Oh, OK,' replies Marty, 'I'll see you later'.

So he scampers off towards the home of Wallace worm.

Upon arrival, he bangs on the front door.

'Can I come in Wallace?' he asks.

'No, go away' cries Wallace, 'I haven't finished my kite yet'.

Marty says goodbye and goes in search of Lucy Ladybird.

She is also busy working on her design and she also tells me to go away.

'They're all working very hard on their kites, I hope they're not as good as mine' he thought.

After lunch all the competitors assemble in the field at the back of the valley. Stood in the middle of the field is Seymour Seagull. Seymour is the starter and judge for the competition.

Holding a megaphone tight to his lips, Seymour asks for all the entrants in the kite competition to bring their kites and join him in the middle of the field.

Marty, Sheldone, Lucy and Wallace step forward with their kites. Their secret designs are revealed.

Marty's design is triangular in shape
and resembles a wedge of cheese.

Sheldone's kite is circular and has a
large snail shell painted on it.

Whilst Wallace has gone for a kite with
a long thin body and Lucy has designed
a square shaped kite covered in red
and black dots.

Seymour explains the rules.

'Right, boys and girls, when I count to three I want you to release your kites' he announces. 'The winner will be the person whose kite climbs the highest'.

'One, two, three, release your kites' he screams.

Suddenly the sky is full of wonderfully coloured shapes.

Each competitor pulls on their kite's string in an attempt to make them climb higher.

The kites respond by flying back and forth, going up and down and some even loop the loop.

'Wow! Look at mine!' shouts Lucy.

'Mine is higher than yours' shouts Wallace as he struggles to control his kite in the breeze.

Sheldone doesn't have any luck at all, his kite is too heavy and after a few twists and turns it comes crashing to the ground.

'You won't be winning this year,' cries Marty.

The wind blows stronger, so strong in fact that it causes Wallace's kite to collide with Lucy's and they both fall to the ground.

'Sorry Lucy' shouts Wallace apologetically.

Realising his is the only kite left in the sky Marty begins to celebrate.

'Yahoo' he shouts.

26

He lets go of one of his kite strings and punches the air in triumph.

'I'm the winner' he shouts.

And he begins dancing and jumping around.
He's so busy celebrating that he

doesn't realise that he is being raised into the air.

'HELP!' he cries looking down at the ground.

'Hold on Marty, we're coming' says Sheldone.

He instructs Wallace to climb on his shell.

'See if you can reach him' he orders.

Wallace tries but he can't quite reach.

'Lucy, climb on my shoulders' shouts Wallace.

Lucy tries her best to reach Marty but the little mouse is out of reach.
'I can't reach him' she cries.
'Stand aside everyone' commands Seymour, and with a big flap of his wings he takes to the air.

He climbs higher and higher until he's alongside the frightened little mouse.

'Am I glad to see you' says Marty.

'Right, Marty, I want you to be a brave mouse and let go of your kite'.

Marty looks down at the ground and gulps.

'If I let go I'll fall' he said.

'No you won't' said Seymour reassuring him. 'Let go and I will catch you'.

'Do you promise?' asks the nervous mouse.

'Just trust me' replied Seymour. 'Now let go'.

Marty shuts his eyes and does as he's told.

Seconds later, Seymour swoops beneath him and the little mouse lands safely on his back.

'Thank you Seymour' says a relieved Marty.

'You're welcome' Seymour replies.

'Now hold on tight' he adds.

Marty nervously grabs hold of Seymour's neck.

Seymour once again changes direction and moments later they both land safely back on the ground.

Everybody is cheering and clapping.

Marty thanks Seymour for coming to his rescue.

'That's what friends are for' replied Seymour.

And he announces Marty the winner of the competition.

Hattie presents Marty with the large corn and berry cake.

'Here you go Marty, I bet you could eat this after that ordeal' says Hattie.

Marty nods in agreement.

'We're all winners today' declares Marty offering a piece of cake to all of his friends.

Buster's blues.

Marty was out enjoying his early morning stroll.

The sun was out and the birds were singing and all seemed well in the valley.

Until he heard a very sad noise.

Someone or something wasn't as happy as he was.

Curious he made his way through the tall grass until he came to an opening by the river. There in front of him, lying on the ground, was a dark figure and the figure was very unhappy.

'Are you OK?' asked Marty.

There was no reply.

Marty crept a little closer.

'I say, are you OK?' he asked again.

This time the sad figure heard him and slowly turned to face him.

Marty could see it was Buster the farmer's dog.

'What's the matter Buster?' he asked.

Sobbing, Buster informs him that he has lost his favourite toy, his ball.

'Don't upset yourself Buster,' replied Marty.

'But you don't understand Marty, It's my favourite toy' sobbed Buster, 'I was having so much fun playing with it but now I've lost it' he adds and starts sobbing again.

'There, there Buster, I'll help you find it' said Marty.

His offer of help brings a smile to Buster's face.

'That's better' said Marty, 'Let's start looking, why don't you check the bushes and I'll check in the long grass'.

Buster sniffs all around, he sniffs the ground, he sniffs the bushes and he even sniffs the trees but there's still no sign of his ball.

'It's no use, I've lost it for good' he weeps.

'Don't worry, we'll find it, we just need some help. Come on follow me' says Marty running off into the woods.

Buster follows.

Soon they arrive at Lucy's house and luckily for them she is out in her garden talking to Wallace and Sheldone.

'Morning Marty' she says greeting him.

'Morning' replies Marty, 'Can you help us?' he asks.

'Who's us?' asks Wallace.
Marty points towards the sad figure of Buster.

'My friend has lost his ball and we can't find it. Will you help us look for it?'.

'Of course we'll help' said Lucy.

'Thank you' barked Buster excitedly wagging his tail.

'Where did you have it last?' asked Wallace.

Buster points to the top of the hill.

'I was up there' replied Buster.

'I threw the ball into the air and when it landed on the ground it rolled down the hill and I haven't seen it since' he sobbed again.

'Don't upset yourself Buster, we'll find it ' assures Sheldone.

Wallace has an idea.

'Why don't we pretend to be a ball and roll ourselves down the hill then maybe one of us will end up next to it' he suggests.

'That's a good idea' agreed Sheldone.

They make their way to the top of the hill and one by one they roll themselves down it. They all end up in a big heap at the bottom.

'Has anyone found it?' asks Buster.

'No' came the reply.

Marty is sat rubbing his sore head when he hears a strange noise.

'Can anyone else hear that ?' he asked.

'I can hear something strange' replies Sheldone.

'What is it?' asks Wallace.

The strange noise was getting closer and closer.

Quack, quack, quack' went the noise.

'Look over there,' shouts Lucy pointing towards the river.

Swimming in their direction is Daisy duck and she is pushing something with her bill.

'Quack, has anyone lost a ball?' she asks.

'I have' shouts Buster.

Lucy realises what has happened.

'The ball must have rolled into the river' she said.

'That's why you couldn't find it Buster' adds Marty.

Daisy brings the ball to the waters edge.

'Here you go Buster' she says pushing the ball towards him.

Buster barks and picks up the dripping wet ball.

Shaking his ball excitedly, he soaks the others.

'Sorry' said Buster apologising.

Just then a familiar voice can be heard calling Buster's name.

'Buster, Buster, where are you boy?' calls the voice.

Buster recognises it straight away. The voice belongs to his master, the farmer.

'I have to go now' he barks and he thanks them again for all their help.

'I'm so glad we could help him' said Lucy.

The
Snow monster.

Marty's head slowly appeared from under his duvet.

'Brr' he thought, 'It's too cold to get up yet, I think I'll have another five minutes sleep'.
So he disappeared back inside his nice warm bedding.

Downstairs, his Mum had just placed a bowl of hot porridge on the kitchen table.

'Time to get up, sleepyhead' she shouts up the stairs.

Reluctantly Marty crawls out of bed.

The cold morning air makes him shiver.

'Come on' shouts his Mum, 'Sheldone will be here soon'.

After washing, Marty goes downstairs and sits at the kitchen table.

'Make sure you it eat that all up' said his Mum pointing to the porridge, 'You're going to need that today'.

Blowing the steam off the porridge Marty asks his Mum why is it so cold today.

'I assume you haven't looked out of the window yet this morning' she said.

Marty walks over to the window.
He wipes the condensation off the
glass and notices the white landscape
outside.

'Cool' he shouts, 'It's snowed, I love

the snow'.

His jubilation is cut short by a knock on
the door.

Marty opens it and is instantly hit in
the face by a freshly made snowball.

'Gotcha' laughs Sheldone.

'Oh, Sheldone' scorns Marty wiping the wet snow off his face.

'Wallace and I are going to build a sledge, would you like to help us?' Sheldone asks.

'That sounds like fun' replies Marty, 'I'll just grab my coat'.

'You're not going anywhere young man, not until you've eaten your breakfast', interrupts his Mum.

'But Mum' says Marty.

'No buts Mister, sit down and eat' she orders.

Not to upset her Marty does as he's told.

When he's finished he grabs his hat and coat and informs his Mum that he'll be back in time for lunch.

'Where are we meeting Wallace?' he asks Sheldone.

'Wallace is at home' replies Sheldone, 'He's already started building the sledge'.

When they arrive, they find him Wallace adding the finishing touches to the sledge.

'What took you so long?' asks Wallace shivering.
'Sorry Wallace, I had to wait for Marty to finish his breakfast' replied Sheldone.

Wallace hasn't had any breakfast and the mention of food makes his tummy rumble.

'What did you have for breakfast, Marty?' he enquires.

'Mum made me a steaming hot bowl of porridge' Marty replied.

The thought of the hot porridge makes Wallace's tummy rumble again.

'The sledge looks great' says Sheldone changing the subject.

'One bit left to fit' says Wallace fitting the brake lever.

'Can we take it for a ride' asks Marty.

'Of course we can, jump on' says Wallace.

Sheldone asks to be the driver and takes his place at the front, Wallace sits in the middle and is in charge of brakes whilst Marty is sat at the back and he's to provide all the power.

Marty digs his heels into the soft snow and gives the sledge a shove. It moves slowly, so he tries again, this time the sledge picks up a bit of momentum.

'Here we go' shouts Sheldone.

They make it to the top of the hill.

'One last push Marty' asks the driver.

Marty digs his heels in again and gives the sledge one final heave and slowly the sledge heads downhill.

But it gradually begins to pick up speed.

'Here we go' shouts Sheldone.

'Wow, this is great fun' shouts Wallace.

'Yahoo' cries Marty.

As they approach Hattie's house they see her shovelling snow in her front garden.

'Good morning' they shout as they whizz past.

Hattie looks up but there's no one there, all that is left is a dusting of snow in the air.

The sledge is now travelling at great speed.

'Watch out for that rock' shouts Wallace.

Sheldone tries to avoid the huge boulder but it's too late.

Hitting the rock the sledge is thrown off course. It is now heading towards the river.

'Slam on the brakes, Wallace!' commands Sheldone.

Wallace pulls on the brake lever but the lever snaps off in his hand.

'I can't slow us down' he shouts waving the broken lever in the air.

'See what you can do Marty' asks Wallace.
Marty digs his heels into the snow but no matter how hard he tries he cannot slow the sledge down.

'Get ready for a soaking' shouts Sheldone as they hurtle towards the river.

Wallace grabs hold of Sheldone and Marty grabs hold of Wallace.

'Here we go' yells Sheldone.

And the sledge hits the water.

Surprisingly they don't get soaked.
Then they realise that the river has frozen over.

As they hit the ice, the sledge spins out of control. Sheldone does his best to keep control of it.

But struggles to do so.
The sledge narrowly misses Lucy who is on the ice, skating.

Trying to act cool, Marty waves to her but is instantly thrown from the sledge.

Wallace tries to grab hold of him but he is thrown off the sledge also.

Sheldone is left fighting for control as he and the sledge head for the bank on the far side.

The sledge crashes into the base of an old oak tree and is covered in fallen snow.

There's no sign of the sledge and no sign of Sheldone.

Concerned, Lucy skates over and checks on Marty.

'Are you OK?' she asks.

'I think so' replies Marty a little shaken.

She then checks on Wallace.

'Are you hurt?' she asks.

'Just a few scratches' he replies wiping snow off his body.

'Has anyone seen Sheldone?' asked Marty.

They notice that the sledge tracks end at the base of a large pile of snow on the far bank. Cautiously they make there way across the ice.

'Sheldone, Sheldone, where are you?' they call.

Suddenly the large pile of snow begins to move.

'Blimey' yells Lucy, 'It's a snow monster'.

The pile of snow moves towards them.

Scared, Lucy holds onto Wallace.

'He doesn't scare me' says Marty.

He picks up a broken branch and
charges towards the monster.

'Take that' he says, poking the monster
in the stomach.

'Ouch' cries the monster.

'Hang on a minute' says Wallace,

'Snow monsters don't say ouch'.

Marty pokes the monster again.

A large pile of snow falls to the floor.

The monsters identity is revealed.

'Oh, Sheldone! I thought you were a real monster' said Lucy.

'Me? a monster?' said Sheldone.

'Yes you' they reply laughing.

'I'm glad you're not' says Lucy giving him a big hug, 'You're freezing'.

'I know what you need' said Marty, 'You need a bowl of my Mum's hot porridge'.

Wallace's tummy rumble again.

'I'll ask her to make you some too Wallace' laughs Marty.

Lucy's
big surprise.

It's a very special day in the valley,

because today it's Lucy Ladybirds birthday.

And like most excited people on their birthday she is waiting for her birthday cards to arrive.

Suddenly there's a knock on the door.

She runs to open it and standing there, in his red and blue uniform, is Percy the postal Pigeon.

'Morning Lucy, happy birthday to you' says Percy as he hands her a bundle of cards.

'Thank you, Percy' she replies and she takes her cards inside and puts them on the table.

Sitting at the table the first card she opens is from Sheldone, he has written 'Happy birthday Princess' inside it, this makes her feel very special.

The next card she opens is from Wallace, followed by further cards from Hattie, Seymour and Percy.

Displaying them on the mantle piece she counts them.

'One, two, three, four, five, six..' she realises that she hasn't received a card from Marty.

'It's not like him to forget my birthday' she thought.

At that moment there's another knock on the door.

'That must be him now ' she thought to herself.Opening the door she expects to see Marty stood there, but he isn't, instead there's a large bunch of flowers on her doorstep.

She bends down to pick them up and suddenly Wallace appears from behind them.

'Happy birthday Lucy' he shouts.

'Thank you Wallace' replies Lucy and she invites him inside for a cup of tea.

'I'm sorry' replies Wallace, 'I can't stop, I have something very important to do' and he leaves.

She thanks him again for the lovely flowers and takes them inside.

65

She is busy arranging them in a vase when there's another knock on the door.

This time it's Sheldone.

'Happy birthday' he shouts presenting her with a large box of chocolates.

'Thank you Sheldone, would you like a cup of nettle tea?' she asks.

'Sorry Lucy, I can't stop, I'm working on something very important' he says and he waves her goodbye.

'That's funny', she thought, 'Why is everyone so busy today'.
There's a further knock on the door.

She opens it to find Hattie stood their holding a pink gift-wrapped parcel.

'Here you go Lucy' she says handing her the box. 'It's a special present for a special person'.

Lucy opens the box expecting to find her birthday cake, but It's not a cake, instead Hattie has made her a beautiful, sparkly tiara.

'Happy birthday' says Hattie placing the tiara on Lucy's head.

Lucy takes a look at herself in the mirror.

Seeing the disappointment on her face Hattie asks her if she likes her present.

'Of course I do' replies Lucy, 'But I was expecting it to be my birthday cake'.

'I thought we'd agreed that Marty was in charge of making your cake this year' Hattie replied.

'We did agree' said Lucy, 'The trouble is I think he has forgotten It's my birthday'.
'I'm sure he hasn't forgotten' assures Hattie , 'I expect he's overslept, I'll go and find him for you'.

Lucy thanks her and shows her out.

She is admiring the tiara in the mirror again when there's another knock on the door.

'Who is it?' she shouts.

'It's me, Marty' came the reply.

She runs over to the front door and opens it. Seymour is stood there puffing and panting.

'Happy birthday Lucy' he says, 'I would have been here earlier but this box was extremely heavy'.

Lucy's not listening to him, she is too busy looking for someone else.

'Who are you looking for?' asks Seymour.

'I thought I heard Marty's voice' she replied.

Realising he isn't there she bends down to pick up the box.

Seymour stops her.

'I'm sorry Lucy but you can't have your present until all you friends are here', he says.

'But that's the trouble' says Lucy, 'Marty has forgotten and everybody else is too busy'.

At this point Marty bursts out of the box holding a large cream birthday cake.

'Surprise Lucy' he shouts.

'Oh, Marty, I thought you'd forgotten'
said a relieved Lucy.

'I'm sorry Lucy but I wanted it to be a
big surprise' he said.
Suddenly three heads appear from
behind a nearby bush. It's Sheldone,
Wallace and Hattie.

'What are you doing here? I thought you were all busy today' said Lucy.

'We have been' they reply, 'We've been helping Marty with your cake'.

Lucy now understands why nobody wanted any nettle tea.

They join in and sing happy birthday to her.

'Thank you all very much' said Lucy, 'This has to be the best birthday surprise ever'.

The tales of Marty mouse.

Printed in Great Britain
by Amazon